D0677636

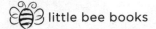 little bee books

An imprint of Bonnier Publishing USA
251 Park Avenue South, New York, NY 10010
Copyright © 2017 by Bonnier Publishing USA
All rights reserved, including the right of reproduction in whole or in part in any form. Little Bee Books is a trademark of Bonnier Publishing USA, and associated colophon is a trademark of Bonnier Publishing USA.

Library of Congress Cataloging-in-Publication Data is available upon request.

Printed in the United States of America LB 0917
ISBN 978-1-4998-0476-8 (hc)
First Edition 10 9 8 7 6 5 4 3 2 1
ISBN 978-1-4998-0475-1 (pb)
First Edition 10 9 8 7 6 5 4 3 2 1
littlebeebooks.com
bonnierpublishingusa.com

ELLA AND OWEN

DRAGON SPIES!

by
Jaden Kent

little bee books

illustrated by
Iryna Bodnaruk

TABLE OF CONTENTS

① THE DARK CAVE OF DARKNESS

Dragon twins Ella and Owen plopped onto the dark, cold ground of the cave.

"This is all your fault!" Ella said.

"How is this my fault?" Owen replied.

"If you hadn't hit your head on that branch, I wouldn't have tried to help you and we wouldn't have fallen into this dark cave," Ella said. "I think I bent my tail."

2

Ella felt a root poking out from the side of the cavern. She lit it with her fire breath. Light flickered around the room.

Owen screamed, "Noooo!"

Tall, creepy, hand-carved wooden statues of fierce warrior dwarves holding shovels lined the large underground chamber.

"I don't want to see this!" Owen patted on the root with his tail to put out the fire. The chamber was dark again.

"Don't be such a baby," an annoyed Ella said. She lit the root again.

"Nooooo!" Owen screamed, able to see the dwarf statues again. He blew out the flame. The chamber was dark once more.

"Would you *please* stop doing that?" Ella snapped.

"Not until those creepy statues go away!" Owen replied.

Ella took a deep breath, ready to light the root one more time, but she stopped and let out a puff of steam instead.

BA-DOOM-BOOM!

"Did you hear that?" she asked.

"Hear what?" Owen replied.

BA-DOOM-BOOM-BOOM!

"That!" Ella pointed down the dark cavern.

BA-DOOM-BOOM-BA-DOOM!

"It sounds like drums. And drums mean that someone down that dark tunnel is going to come out and try to eat us," Owen explained. "So let's get out of here!"

"Let's go check it out," Ella urged.

"Oh no," replied Owen. He shook his head. "Drums being played in a dark underground cavern never ends in anything good."

"Don't be such a scary baby," Lila said. "I'm going to go take a look. It might be a way out of here." She fluttered her wings and flew toward the sound of the drums.

Owen sighed and followed her. "This will only end in tears," he said. "Probably mine."

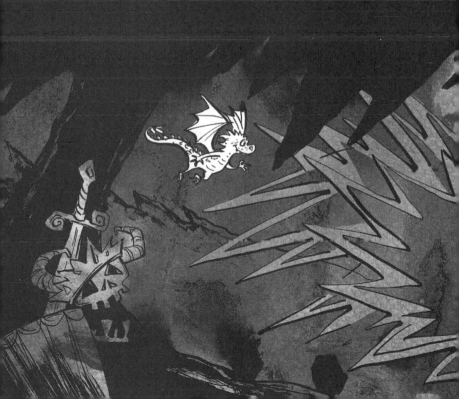

The two dragons flew down the long tunnel. They entered a well-lit chamber where two bearded dwarves danced in a circle. A third bearded dwarf pounded on two short tribal drums. The dwarves' hairy bare feet poked out from underneath blue overalls. Their scraggly hair needed a comb. Their noses were large and took up most of their faces.

The drumming dwarf stopped playing and pointed to Ella and Owen at the entrance.

"Intruders!" he shouted.

"Score update!" Owen told Ella. "Evil drums: one. My sister who never listens to me: zero!"

"Get them!" The three dwarves charged toward Ella and Owen.

"Aha! Now we've got you!" One of the dwarves poked a shovel at Ella and Owen. "My name's Jumpy the Dwarf!"

The two dragons stood with their backs against the cave wall. Jumpy pointed to the other two dwarves. "And these are my brothers, Lumpy and Stumpy. Say hello, brothers!"

"Hello, elf spies!" Lumpy said.

"Elf spies?! Oh no! We're not elf spies," Ella replied. "We're dragons."

Jumpy laughed. "Ha-ha! Only elf spies would claim that they're not elf spies, and that proves that you're both elf spies *disguised* as dragons!"

"Dwarves are very good at logic!" Lumpy said.

"And we're also very good at knowing when someone has come to steal our dirt!" Stumpy said.

"Why would we steal your dirt?" Owen asked.

"Because *everyone* wants dirt!" Jumpy scoffed. "Triple-winged fire flamingos. Swamp baboons. And especially lying, dirt-thieving elves and their spies." He looked directly at Ella and Owen.

"I still don't understand why we would want your dirt," Ella said.

"Because dirt is amazing!" Stumpy replied.

"Look at all the things you can do with it," Lumpy said. "You can use it to make things dirty . . . you can shovel it . . . with a shovel."

"You can pile it. In a pile," Jumpy added. "And you can . . . you can . . . you can use it to make things dirty. . . ."

"You already said that one," Ella pointed out.

"If you don't understand the value of dirt, it's not our job to explain it to you!" Lumpy sneered.

Owen tapped Ella on the shoulder. "We'll be going now," he said to the dwarves. "Since we don't know much about dirt, we can't possibly be elf spies. That's dragon logic."

"Not so fast," Jumpy said. He shook his shovel in the air. It poked into the roof of the cavern, knocking dirt onto his long beard. "For trying to steal dwarf dirt, we dwarves sentence you to . . . to . . ."

"Bake us cookies!" Lumpy said. "It's nearly time for third snack."

"Scratch our beards," Stumpy said, "to get rid of our cave fleas."

"That's so *gross*," Ella said.

"At least you're not going to eat us," Owen added.

"*That's* so gross," Jumpy said.

"Dragons are so salty and scaly," Lumpy observed.

"I'd rather have my beard scratched," Stumpy added, scratching his beard until a cave flea hopped out of it.

Ella spoke up. "I'm not scratching any—"

"Silence!" Jumpy yelled. "The Dwarf King will know what to do with elf spies!"

"To the Dwarf King!" the three dwarves yelled.

"Did you hear that, Ella?" Owen said. "We're going to meet the king!"

3

IN THE HALL OF THE DWARF KING

"So, you have brought me elf spies?" the Dwarf King asked. "Excellent!"

He sat on a large throne carved out of dirt. A crown made from an old leather hat sat on top of his head. In his right hand, he held a golden shovel. It was so shiny he could see his reflection in the blade.

"We're not elf spies," Owen said. "Not, not, not!"

"We already explained that to Bumpy, Slumpy, and Dumpy." Ella pointed to the three dwarves.

"I'm Stumpy!" Stumpy said. "And *he's* Jumpy, and *he's* Lumpy!"

"And we're not elf spies!" Ella repeated.

"Aha!" The Dwarf King pointed a hairy finger at the two dragons. "Only elf spies would say that they're not elf spies, proving that you're both elf spies!" the Dwarf King said. "I'm very good at dwarf logic."

The Dwarf King held up his shovel and used it to pick out a piece of speckled turkey meat stuck between his two front teeth.

"The Dwarf King has spoken!" Jumpy yelled.

"Elf spies! Elf spies! Elf spies!" Lumpy and Stumpy chanted.

"And we can prove it!" Jumpy said. He and Lumpy grabbed Owen's tail and pulled. "Once we get these disguises off them, that is. Pull!"

"I'm pulling!" Lumpy said.

"Hey!" Owen yelped. "These aren't costumes!"

"Yes, they are," Stumpy said. He grabbed one of Ella's wings. "And they'll come right off, elf spy!"

Ella quickly spun around, making Stumpy let go and crash into a wall. Her tail whipped past Owen and smacked Jumpy and Lumpy. The dwarves let go of Owen's tail and fell backward onto the ground.

"These aren't disguises!" Owen said.

"We really are dragons!" Ella added.

"Dragons who spy for the elves and are here to steal our dirt!" the Dwarf King shouted.

"Why does everyone think we want to steal your dirt?" Owen asked. "It's just . . . dirt!"

"If you don't understand the value of dirt, it's not my job to explain it to you," the Dwarf King said.

"Dirt has no value," Ella pointed out. "It's dirt."

"And you are wrong, elf spy," the Dwarf King said, laughing. "We are building Mud Pie Gigantus, the kingdom's largest mud pie. We plan to drop it on our most hated enemies."

"Is that the elves?" Owen asked.

"Of course!" the Dwarf King said. "Elves are leaf-huggers and plant-petters and they live in trees instead of dark caves like the best of us do. And, worst of all, they *don't* have any dirt—which is why they want to steal all of ours!"

The Dwarf King pointed to a large pie plate nearby filled with mud. "So we're gonna splat them out of their forest!"

The Dwarf King stood up. He waved his golden shovel in the air. "Jumpy! Lumpy! Stumpy!" the Dwarf King barked. "Throw these elf spies into our dirt mine. We need them to dig dirt for the rest of their elf spy lives."

"At least they didn't eat us!" Owen said. "Our luck is changing."

"Shoveling dirt for the rest of our lives is not much of an improvement," Ella replied.

"Stop talking in your elf spy code, elf spies, and start digging!" Jumpy said.

Stumpy handed each dragon a shovel. "Welcome to our dirt mine. It's shovel time!"

"Wow! New shovels!" Owen said. "And mine's shinier than yours!"

Ella looked around the cold, damp dirt mine. A long tunnel with a light at the end of it led away from the mining cave. That had to be the way out, she thought, but it seemed so far away.

"We have to get out of here," Ella whispered. "We need to find the elves and warn them that these crazy dwarves are going to drop a giant mud pie on them."

"No way! This place is great!" Owen said. "Look what I made!"

Owen pointed to a mud castle he'd made in the dirt.

"Stop playing and dig," Lumpy ordered.

"If I wanted to do chores instead of play, I would've just stayed home," Owen whined. He dumped a shovelful of dirt into a wheelbarrow. "My wings ache already."

"Don't worry. I have a plan," Ella whispered. She checked to make sure the three dwarves weren't watching. They were squished together on a wooden bench, getting ready to nap. Jumpy, Lumpy, and Stumpy closed their eyes.

"Oh no!" Ella cried out.

The dwarves' eyes snapped open and they sat up straight. "What, what, what?" they cried out.

Ella held up her empty shovel with her claws. "Elves! It was the elves! They just stole all my fresh dirt!"

Jumpy, Lumpy, and Stumpy threw their short arms into the air and ran around in circles in a panic. They banged into one another and fell to the ground.

"Sound the dirt alarm!" cried Jumpy. He held up a large cowbell.

"Don't ring it!" Ella yelled. "If you sound the alarm, the elves'll know you're coming! You'd have a better chance of catching them if you just run after them!"

"Good idea," Lumpy said. "Let's go!"

Jumpy, Lumpy, and Stumpy raced down the tunnel after the imaginary elves. When the dwarves were gone, Ella jumped into a pile of mud.

"Come on!" she said to Owen. "We've got to disguise ourselves."

Owen followed her lead and they quickly rolled in the mud, covering their bodies.

They tiptoed down the tunnel, sneakily following the dwarves toward the exit. Jumpy, Lumpy, and Stumpy stood at the tunnel's entrance, shaking their tiny fists in the air.

"The elf spies got away!" Lumpy said.

"They've gone to warn their elf masters," Jumpy added.

"We have to tell the Dwarf King," Stumpy said.

The dwarves turned to go back into the dirt mine and froze. Ella and Owen stood in front of them, covered in mud.

"We are the monsters of mud!" Ella groaned. "You have been taking our dirt!"

"Now we're gonna turn *you* into mud!" Owen groaned.

The dwarves smiled.

"Yay! We love mud!" Stumpy cheered.

"Do it! Do it! Do it!" yelled Lumpy.

"We mean, uh, we're going to stuff you in our muddy mouths and eat you!" Owen said.

"AAAAAAAAAAH!" the three dwarves screamed in fear. They ran down the tunnel past Ella and Owen and into the mine.

"Come on! Let's get out of here and warn the elves!" Ella said.

"Aw, can't we go scare those three dwarves a little more first?" Owen asked.

"Please?"

"Okay, but just a bit," Ella agreed.

Owen and Ella ran after Jumpy, Lumpy, and Stumpy. "GRRRRRR!" they yelled.

"This is the most fun I've had in days!" Owen said to his sister.

5

MAY THE FOREST BE WITH YOU

"Chasing those crazy dwarves was more fun than throwing pixie dust on an angry ogre!" Owen laughed as they soared through the sky. He laughed so hard that his tail shook.

"Well, playtime's over. We've gotta warn the elves!" Ella folded her wings against her body and dove toward the forest where the elves lived.

"I can't wait to meet a real elf!" Owen said, diving next to his sister. "They've got pointy ears and pointy noses and pointy shoes and pointy hats and—LOOK!"

Owen shouted so loudly, Ella's tail curled up.

"Why're you shouting, scale brains?!" Ella snapped.

"Look! Look! Look!" Owen repeated. "ELVES!"

Owen pointed to three elves marching back and forth along a thick tree branch. The elves were dressed in green shorts with green suspenders and white shirts. They wore pointy green shoes and pointy green hats. And, exactly as Owen had hoped, they had pointy ears and long, pointy noses.

The two dragons landed next to them on their branch.

"I'm Owen!" Owen announced. "And this is my sister—"

"DWARF SPIES!" one of the elves shouted, pointing at them.

"Uh, no. Her name is Ella," Owen said.

"We know you're dwarf spies!" A second elf poked Ella with a twig. "Grab a twig and start poking these spies, Jingle!"

"We're not dwarf spies," Ella said and smacked the twig away.

"Aha! Only dwarf spies would claim that they're not dwarf spies, proving that you're both dwarf spies! Isn't that right, Juggle?" the elf named Jingle said with a sneer.

"By the point of my pointy nose, that's right!" Juggle said. "You've come to steal our leaves, haven't you?!"

Jingle grabbed a handful of leaves from the tree and stuffed them into his pockets.

"Why would we steal your leaves?" Owen asked. "Because everyone wants leaves!" the last elf, who was named Jangle, scoffed.

"Look at all the things you can do with leaves," Jingle began. "You can use them to make a leaf pile . . . you can rake them . . . you can look at them . . . you can . . . you can . . . you can use them to make a leaf pile. . . ."

"You already said that one," Ella pointed out.

"If you don't understand the value of leaves, it's not our job to explain it to you," Jingle huffed.

"What should
we do with them?"
Juggle asked.
"I say we take 'em
to the queen and let
her decide," Jingle said.

"Yeah! We get to meet the Elf Queen!" Owen cheered and excitedly thumped his tail on the branch. "Oooh! I hope her crown is pointy!"

The Elf Queen sat on a large throne made of branches and leaves in the middle of an ornate hut high atop a tree. She was taller than the other elves. Her clothes were red and, much to Owen's delight, she wore a pointy crown with a bell on top that tinkled every time she moved her head.

Jingle, Jangle, and Juggle led Ella and
Owen before the queen.

"I'm Owen, Your Pointy-ness!" Owen
announced. "And this is my sister—"

"DWARF SPIES!" the Elf Queen shouted.
The bell on her crown tinkled.

"Uh, no. Her name is Ella," Owen said to the Elf Queen. Then he whispered to Ella, "Why does everyone think your name is Dwarf Spies?"

Ella stepped toward the Elf Queen. Jingle and Jangle, standing at attention in front of the queen, immediately crossed branches like swords to stop her.

"We're not dwarf spies, Your Highness," Ella said.

"Aha! Only dwarf spies would claim that they're not dwarf spies, proving that you're both dwarf spies!" the Elf Queen accused.

56

"We came here to warn you that the dwarves are planning to drop a giant mud pie on you," Owen explained.

"You're not very good dwarf spies if you come here and tell us all your dwarf plans," the Elf Queen said.

"That's because we're *not* dwarf spies!" Ella flapped her wings in frustration. "We're dragons!"

"Or . . . are you dwarves *dressed* as dragons so you can steal our leaves?!" the Elf Queen asked.

"This just keeps getting crazier and crazier," Owen said to Ella. "Can we please go home now?"

"Will you still think we're crazy when we drop *this* on your dwarf tunnels?!" The Elf Queen pointed to a huge ball made of leaves.

"Why do you want to drop a giant leaf ball on the dwarves?" Ella asked.

"Because you dwarves are dirt-lovers who live in dark caves and not in trees and you don't have any leaves—which is why you want to steal *our* leaves!" the Elf Queen explained.

"Makes sense to me," Owen said with a shrug.

"We'll just be running along now and leave you crazy elves to drop all the leaves you want on the crazy dwarves," Ella said.

But before the dragons could flap their wings, the Elf Queen rose from her throne and shook a fistful of leaves over her head.

"We must teach these dwarf spies a lesson! Something awful! Something terrible! Something to make dwarves think twice about messing with us elves!" she proclaimed.

Ella and Owen huddled closer as their scales trembled.

"Throw them into the leaf dungeon and make them rake leaves for the rest of their lives!" the Elf Queen announced.

Ella stopped trembling. "What's so awful about raking leaves?"

"We make you do it with a *very* small rake," Jangle explained.

"**B**oy, those nutty elves weren't kidding. This thing is smaller than a baby gnome." Owen struggled to hold a small rake with his claws.

"I don't think it matters how big the rake is. We'll never be able to rake all these leaves!" Ella pointed to a towering pile of leaves so high that it blocked out the sun.

"Wheeeeee!" Jingle, Jangle, and Juggle cheered as they jumped up and down atop the huge leaf pile. Leaves scattered in all directions.

Owen's wings sagged. He'd have to rake them into the pile all over again. "Looks like we'll never get to eat Mom's prickle slime slug pie again," he sighed.

"Stop trying to cheer me up," Ella said. "Besides, we're not going to be here for the rest of our lives. I've got a plan."

Ella used a leaf to tickle Owen's nose.

"AH-CHOOOOOO!"

Owen let out a huge dragon sneeze that blew over the leaf tower. Leaves flew everywhere like snowflakes in a blizzard atop Thunderstorm Mountain.

"Leaf-alanche!" Jangle shouted as he, Jingle, and Juggle tumbled down from the top of the collapsing leaf pile.

Ella and Owen raced away as the elves were buried under a pile of leaves.

"The dwarf spies are escaping!" Juggle shouted once he could poke his head out from the leaf pile.

It was too late. Ella and Owen flew up and above the trees before the elves could reach them.

"We've gotta warn the dwarves that the elves are going to drop a giant leaf ball on them!" Owen said.

"And get captured again as elf spies? I'd rather eat prickle slime slug pie," Ella replied.

"Well, you'd better think of something quick because we've got company!" Owen said.

The Dwarf King, Jumpy, Lumpy, and Stumpy were flying toward them on a wooden, four-seated flying bicycle with wings. Their peddling spun an airplane propeller attached to the back and kept them bobbing across the sky. Hanging below the bike was their huge mud pie.

"We've gotta stop them!" Ella said.

"If we stop the dwarves, then who's gonna stop *them*?" Owen said, pointing back to the elves, who were now airborne.

The Elf Queen, Jingle, Jangle, and Juggle peddled toward them on their own crazy flying machine. Below them hung their huge leaf ball.

8

FLYING THE UNFRIENDLY SKIES

"**S**plit up!" Owen called out as he turned to fly toward the elves.

Ella raced toward the dwarves, but she wasn't exactly sure what she would do once she got to them.

"You've got to stop!"
Owen called out to
the Elf Queen. "Dropping
giant leaf balls on everyone
different from you isn't very nice!"

"Out of our way, dwarf spy!" the Elf Queen shouted and threw a handful of leaves at Owen. The leaves smacked him in the face.

"Ack! Leaves taste yucky!" Owen said, spitting them from his mouth.

Jingle and Jangle swung branches at him.

"You better *leaf* us alone!" Jangle yelled at Owen, then looked to Jingle and said, "Get it? *Leaf* us alone?"

Ella wasn't doing much better.

"You've got to turn back! Dropping a mud pie on the elves will only make things worse!" Ella called out.

"Get out of our way, elf spy!" the Dwarf King shouted and threw mud at Ella.

The mud splattered on Ella's scales.

"Ugh! And I just took a bath last month!" Ella growled.

Jingle, Jangle, and Juggle threw more leaves at Owen while Jumpy, Lumpy, and Stumpy flung mud at Ella. The two dragons flapped their wings. They dove, twisted, and spun in the air to avoid the ongoing mud and leaf attack.

"Throw more leaves!" the Elf Queen commanded. "Get those dwarf spies!"

"Throw more mud!" the Dwarf King ordered. "Get those elf spies!"

"How did this go from a battle between elves and dwarves to both sides trying to get us?!" Owen cried.

Lumpy threw his last mud ball at Ella. She dodged his throw, but—**SPLAT!**—flew into another mud ball flung in her direction. Jumpy's mud ball had hit her in the face.

"GAHH!" Ella yelled. She spun to her right and, unable to see where she was flying, smacked into Owen.

"OOOOF!" Owen gasped as he spiraled downward and crashed into the elves' flying machine.

Ella bounced off Owen and smacked into the Dwarf King.

"Ahhh! Elf spy attack!" the Dwarf King shouted. "Abandon ship!"

But it was too late. Unable to control their flying machines, the elves and the dwarves fell from the sky and plopped onto the ground in a big, muddy, leafy mess.

A moment later, Ella and Owen crashed on top of them.

9

HERE'S MUD IN YOUR PIE

Ella, Owen, the elves, and the dwarves were now all covered in leaves and mud. The whole group was piled in a leafy, muddy mess!

"This is all your fault!" the Elf Queen and Dwarf King shouted at Ella and Owen at the same time.

"Capture those dwarves, Jingle!" the Elf Queen shouted to the mud- and leaf-covered creature next to her.

"I'm not Jingle the elf! I'm Lumpy the dwarf!" a mud- and leaf-covered Lumpy replied.

"Throw those elves into the dirt mine!" the Dwarf King ordered the three dwarves next to him.

But they weren't dwarves. They were elves covered with mud and leaves, so it was impossible to tell who was who.

"We're elves!" a mud- and leaf-covered Jangle said to the Dwarf King.

"Where are Jumpy, Lumpy, and Stumpy?!" The Dwarf King huffed and picked leaves from his beard.

"We're over here!" Jumpy said. He was so muddy that no one could tell who he was.

"I thought you were an elf!" the Elf Queen said to Jumpy. Mud dripped from her muddy crown and landed on her pointy nose.

86

"Look at you guys," Owen said. "You've got so much mud and leaves on you, no one can even tell who is who."

"Yeah!" Ella added. "You guys spend all your time fighting over how different you are, but now that you can't tell who is who, you can see that you're really not so different after all . . . at least when you're covered in mud and leaves."

Owen used his tail to scrape a pile of mud off himself and present it to the Elf Queen. "Whaddya say, Queen? Give it a try. . . ."

The Elf Queen paused. She nervously looked at the mud. "But it's so . . . *muddy*."

"That's the whole point!" Owen said.

Owen jumped into the air and landed in the middle of a mud puddle, splashing mud onto Jingle, Jangle, and Juggle. The three elves responded by laughing and playing in the mud.

The Elf Queen picked up a handful of mud and tossed it into a mud pile. "Hey! This is kinda . . . different from what I thought it would be. It's not so bad," she said, surprised.

"And I never realized how pretty leaves are," the equally surprised Dwarf King said, picking a large red leaf out of his beard. "We could use these to decorate our dirt mines. . . ."

"Maybe you guys could spend some time getting to know each other instead of finding new ways to fight each other," Ella suggested.

"I bet the dwarves could show you how to grow an awesome beard if you teach them how to make a pointy hat," Owen said to the elves.

"Ooooh! I've always wanted a pointy hat!" the Dwarf King cheered.

"And we've *always* wanted to grow awesome beards!" Juggle said.

"Good to hear! And now that everything's settled, we'll just be flying on outta here," Ella said and flapped her wings.

"STOP!" the Elf Queen shouted.

Ella and Owen froze mid-flap. "I knew this was all too good to be true," Owen whispered.

"If you're not dwarf spies . . ." the Elf Queen started.

"Or elf spies . . ." the Dwarf King added.

"Who *are* you?" the Elf Queen asked.

"We're just two dragons trying to do the right thing," Ella said.

"*And* trying to get home," Owen added.

"Yeah. That too," Ella agreed.

"Well, thank you for showing us the foolishness of our ways," the Elf Queen said.

"And if you want to get home, maybe this'll help." The Dwarf King reached into his long beard and pulled out a map.

"Boy, will it ever!" Owen said and took the map. "Thanks!"

"No. Thank *you* for showing us that we dwarves and elves aren't so different after all," the Dwarf King replied. He laughed as he threw some leaves into the air.

With the map securely clenched in one of Owen's claws, he and Ella said their goodbyes and soared into the sky. They had seen castles and met knights on this adventure. They had traveled through Terror Swamp. They had visited the underground kingdom of the dwarves and the high treetop palace of the elves, but now they were finally heading toward the one place they wanted to be most of all. . . .

Home.

Read on for a sneak peek from the seventh book in the Ella and Owen series, *Twin Trouble*

"**A**ccording to this map, the Lollipop Forest is this way," Owen said to his twin sister, pointing to his right as they flew toward home. "And way over there is the Evil Pumpkin Patch. And way, way over there, where all the steam is? That's Goblin University, and we're *not* going there."

"No, never, because that steam is from their giant cooking pots," Ella replied. She studied the old map the Dwarf King had given them. "And Dragon Patch should be straight ahead."

Ella and Owen had brought peace to the conflict between the angry dwarves and the excitable elves, and a map showing the dragons how to get back home to Dragon Patch was their reward.

Their wings fluttered rapidly as they flew through the trees.

Owen looked at the map. "I think Dragon Patch is that way, through the Valley of Stones that Look Like Faces," Owen said excitedly. "We're finally going home, and I'm going to go straight to my room."

"What's so great about your room?" Ella asked.

"Two things," said Owen. "First,

it's where all my books are, and I've missed them. And second, it's not *your* room."

"That's because my room is super-dragon awesome, and—wait, did you hear that?" Ella paused to listen.

"No, I totally did not hear anything that sounds like two creatures arguing in the distance," Owen replied.

"Let's go check it out," Ella said.

Owen pointed in the direction they were flying. "But this way leads to my room and my books!" he said. He pointed off in the opposite direction. "And do you know where the other direction leads? To arguing voices."

"Being in your room's even more boring than cleaning the beetle scum from my claws," Ella said. "At least this might be something fun!" She changed direction and flew toward the forest to check out the voices.

"I know I'm gonna regret this." Owen sighed and flew after his sister.

The voices grew louder as the dragons approached a clearing in the forest.

"Are too!" a boy's voice said.

"Are not!" a girl's voice disagreed.

When they got to the clearing, Ella and Owen could see who was arguing. Owen's eyes widened. His jaw dropped open.

"Unicorns!" he excitedly squealed. "They've even got unicorn horns and everything!"

"Uh, *yeah*." Ella yawned. "If they had *two* horns, they'd be called 'two-nicorns.'"

And they weren't *just* unicorns, but *twin* unicorns. Their coats were iridescent and they had beautiful, flowing tails and manes. One unicorn had a shiny gold horn, and the other had a silver horn with rainbow sparkles. They appeared to be about the same age as Ella and Owen.

"I've never seen a unicorn before!" Owen said.

"So amazing," Ella said before pausing. "Are we sure they're friendly?"

"Let's go talk to them!" Owen then had a better idea. "Oooo! Maybe they'll let us ride them!"

Owen happily scampered toward the unicorns.

"I know I'm gonna regret this." Ella sighed and flew after her brother.